To my Queridx J&L, don't forget to stand in front of the mirror
and say, "I am beautiful. I am perfect. I am loved." —N.R.

For Carolina —K.M.

Carolrhoda Books®
An imprint of Lerner Publishing Group, Inc.
241 First Avenue North
Minneapolis, MN 55401 USA

For reading levels and more information, look up this title at www.lernerbooks.com.

Designed by Kimberly Morales.
Main body text set in Mikado.
Typeface provided by HVD fonts.
The illustrations in this book were created with Photoshop and collaged tissue paper.

Library of Congress Cataloging-in-Publication Data

Names: Ramos, NoNieqa, author. | Morris, Keisha, illustrator.
Title: Hair story / NoNieqa Ramos ; illustrations by Keisha Morris.
Description: Minneapolis : Carolrhoda Books, 2021. | Audience: Ages 5–9. | Audience: Grades 2–3. | Summary: Illustrations and rhythmic, rhyming text follow a Boricua girl and a Black girl from birth through early childhood, culminating in a playdate where they celebrate their natural hair.
Identifiers: LCCN 2020049346 (print) | LCCN 2020049347 (ebook) | ISBN 9781541579163 (trade hardcover) | ISBN 9781728417370 (eb pdf)
Subjects: CYAC: Stories in rhyme. | Hair—Fiction. | Puerto Ricans—Fiction. | African Americans—Fiction. | Friendship—Fiction.
Classification: LCC PZ8.3.R1456 Hai 2021 (print) | LCC PZ8.3.R1456 (ebook) | DDC [E]—dc23

LC record available at https://lccn.loc.gov/2020049346
LC ebook record available at https://lccn.loc.gov/2020049347

Manufactured in the United States of America
1-47185-47902-1/26/2021

HAIR STORY

NoNieqa Ramos

Illustrated by **Keisha Morris**

Carolrhoda Books
Minneapolis

Baby's crown,
lush, wild, beautiful brown:
Puerto Rican princesa
perfect lips, belleza.
Perfect skin.
Perfect nose.
Her eyes, just like Abuelo's.

AY BENDITO!

Baby Rudine.
Behold Black royalty!
Hair a wreath of majesty.
Grandmas bestow blessings.
Sing in harmony.
Hallelujahs soar
for the one they adore.

PELO-GROW

Ringlets,
first steps.
Red cap,
ride Papi's back.
Sloppy bun,
basketball fun.
Tresses, kicks, and party dresses.

Pelo malo?
Abuelita calls Preciosa's hair El Huracán.

Peloooow!

Waves the brush like a wand:
FRIZZ BE GONE!

A pelo cyclone,
Abuelita combs and combs.
Pointless,
like trying to straighten out
the ocean.

FRO   NO

Strong hands.
Stubborn knots.
Scalp, tender.
Iron, hot.
Straighten.
Get used to waitin'.

Spritz and spray.
Tug-of-brush.
Is it done yet?
Girl, don't rush.

Slick.
Tight.
Sleek.
Smooth.
Hair, do what I tell you to.

Till the temp hits 102.

PELO-CITY

Then baby hairs
break all the rules.
Do what they were meant to do.
BLOOM!

On the stoop.
Moms getting the scoop.
Girls bored, hearing
blah-blah-blah-blah,
decide to play

HAIR SALON!

Mirror, mirror,
what do you see?
A dope Nubian queen.

HOW FRO CAN

Espejo, espejo, ¿qué ves aquí?
A fly Taíno queen.

Generations of courage
reflected in their eyes,
beauty 4eva multiplied.

YOU GROW?

Moms do each other's dos.

Hair, geometric, electric.
Mathemagic, balanced.

Fingers decode.
Decipher.
Describe.
Uncover the algorithm
inside.

$$(6x-5)(x-2)-(3x-1)(2x-3)=4$$

$$\frac{4}{5}x-2\frac{1}{2}x-2=-2\frac{1}{3}x-\frac{1}{6}-\frac{1}{5}$$

$$\frac{1+16a}{7}=\frac{5a-4}{2}$$

FRO-ZEN

Fingers and rubber bands choreograph.
Hairs dance.
Jeté.
Chassé.
Hooray for braid ballet!
Harmony.
Synchronicity.
Hairs bow. Curtsy.

Then hand in hand,
mano de la mano,
las bellezas stroll
through the barrio.

They see faces framed.
Dark beauty cascades.
Silhouettes of gorgeousness
mirrored in Preciosa's gaze.

FRO-MENTS IN TIME

DIANA AND TRACEE ELLIS ROSS

CHESLIE KRYST

IRIS CHACÓN

EVA DUARTE DE PERÓN

HARRIET TUBMAN

FREDERICK DOUGLASS

SANDRA CISNEROS

AMARIYANNA (MARI) COPENY

PELO

Fruity piraguas.
Brain freeze!
Girls in the grass,
hair ridin' the breeze.

Clouds glide.
Girls read the sky.

Tapestry
of history.
Living.
Everlasting.
Crisscross:
strands of strength
and loss.
Resilience and pride
intertwined.
Woven glory.

HAIR STORY.

FRO-MENTS IN TIME MURAL

This mural celebrates prominent Black, Afro-Latinx, and non-Black Latinx figures known both for their accomplishments and their notable hairstyles.

Dominican American author and National Poetry Slam champion **Elizabeth Acevedo** wrote *The Poet X*, a National Book Award winner. Her novel *With the Fire on High* will be made into a movie! A strand of Elizabeth Acevedo's Hair Story can be found in her spoken word piece, "Hair," in which she expresses love for her natural, curly hair and Black heritage.

Fans of **Iris Chacón** call her La Bomba de Puerto Rico (the Puerto Rican bombshell) and La Vedette de America (America's showgirl) because of her flamboyant singing, dancing, and acting. She starred in the first Latin act ever presented in the famous Radio City Music Hall in New York. Since 1998 she has hosted *Iris Chacón Live*, a radio show about beauty, health, fitness, and nutrition.

Mexican American poet and novelist **Sandra Cisneros** won the PEN/Nabokov Award for Achievement in International Literature in 2019. Her bilingual picture book *Hairs/Pelitos* celebrates the beautiful diversity of Latinx hair.

At the age of eight, **Amariyanna (Mari) Copeny** marched in protests to bring attention to the ongoing water crisis in Flint, Michigan. Lead contamination poisoned the water and made residents very ill. She wrote to President Barack Obama and asked him to visit and "lift people's spirits" and he did. She still fights for water justice and helps kids in her community. In 2018 her GoFundMe campaign sent hundreds of kids to see the movie *Black Panther*! She is a model in GapKids' "Be the Future" campaign, which features youth activists who are changing the world.

In 2015, eleven-year-old **Marley Dias** was tired of reading about "white boys and their dogs." Through her viral campaign #1000BlackGirlBooks, she has collected and donated more than twelve thousand books featuring Black girls as the main character. On social media, she has talked about her hair, saying, "These girls that are watching me, they're watching me in Afros. They're watching me in box braids. . . . And they're seeing that there is so much variety in our hair. . . . Wearing natural hair in any way you choose is super empowering, and you should always take up space with your hair as much as you want to."

Daveed Daniele Diggs is an award-winning actor best known for playing the Marquis de Lafayette and Thomas Jefferson in the musical *Hamilton*. On his appearance, Diggs commented proudly, "I have a very recognizable silhouette."

Frederick Douglass (ca. 1818–February 20, 1895) escaped enslavement in Maryland and became a national leader of the abolitionist movement. He was famous for speeches such as "Self-Made Men" and his memoir *Narrative of the Life of Frederick Douglass, an American Slave*. The most photographed American of the 1800s, Douglass believed photos showed the "essential humanity" of a person and could help change how white people thought about Black people.

Cuban American teen **Emma González** was a student at Marjory Stoneman Douglas High School in 2018 when a gunman killed seventeen of her classmates. In the days following the shooting, she began speaking out as an activist and gun control advocate, including at the March for Our Lives protest in Washington, DC. She first shaved her head in 2017, saying it freed her from the insecurity of worrying about how her hair looked.

Born in Spanish Town, Jamaica, **Grace Jones** is a legendary model, singer, and actor who starred as Amazonian Zula in the 1984 film *Conan the Destroyer*. She is famous for her striking sense of style and radical high-top fade. She said, "I do change roles in life, I live that way. I go feminine, I go masculine. I am both, actually."

Former San Francisco 49ers quarterback **Colin Kaepernick** is known for his protests before football games. In 2016, he began kneeling during the national anthem to protest social injustice and police brutality against Black people. Kaepernick faced criticism for his protests from politicians and fellow athletes. He was featured in Nike's thirtieth anniversary "Just Do It" campaign with the slogan, "Believe in something. Even if it means sacrificing everything."

Frida Kahlo (July 6, 1907–July 13, 1954), one of Mexico's greatest artists, is known especially for her self-portraits. She created more than two hundred paintings including *Self Portrait with Cropped Hair* in which she depicts herself with her long hair cut off and scattered on the floor and *Self Portrait with Braid* in which she has reattached her hair. Kahlo said, "The most important part of the body is the brain. Of my face, I like the eyebrows and eyes."

Cheslie Kryst is a lawyer who earned the Miss USA title in 2019, the first year in which Black women won all three of America's biggest beauty pageants. Kryst is currently a diversity adviser for a law firm and is a correspondent for the TV program *Extra*.

World-renowned Puerto Rican astrologer and television personality **Walter Mercado** (March 9, 1932–November 2, 2019) gave daily horoscopes to 120 million viewers for more than thirty years. With his golden coiffed hair, crystal jewelry, and gem encrusted capes, he encouraged people to be whoever they wanted to be. His signature phrase "con mucho mucho amor" (with much, much love) delivered messages of hope, strength, and love.

Eva Perón (May 7, 1919–July 26, 1952) was born as María Eva Duarte, later became Eva Duarte de Perón, and was often called Eva Perón or simply Evita. When her husband Juan Perón was president of Argentina, she used her power as First Lady to champion the rights of women and poor people. Her best-known hairstyle was bleached blond hair slicked back into a braided chignon (bun).

Diana Ross is the legendary Motown lead singer of the Supremes, one of the world's most successful girl groups of all time. Their hits included "Baby Love" and "Stop! In the Name of Love." Ross was a pioneer of Black natural hair. She said, "I can be a better me than anyone can."

Tracee Ellis Ross, daughter of Diana Ross, is an actor and founder of Pattern Beauty, a hair-care line for curly hair. She said, "Here is my wish and my desire. . . . That we own and know that we are more than our bodies and yet our bodies are these sacred, beautiful, rhythmic houses for us."

Known as the Moses of her people, **Harriet Tubman** (ca. 1823–March 10, 1913) led hundreds of enslaved Black people to freedom on the Underground Railroad. She also served as a Civil War nurse, a scout, and a spy. Tubman was injured as a teen when a white overseer threw a weight at an enslaved man and struck her in the head instead. She said, "My hair had never been combed and it stood out like a bushel basket. . . . I expect that my hair saved my life."

unLOCKing MEANING: A GLOSSARY

abuelita: (AH-bweh-LEE-tah) grandmother

abuelo: (AH-bweh-loh) grandfather

ay bendito: (I ben-DEE-toh) what a blessing

barrio: (BAR-ee-oh) neighborhood

belleza: (BEH-yeh-sah) beauty

Black: (BLAK) refers to people of various population groups who can often trace their lineage to Africa. Black people are often considered to have darker skin but in fact have a wide range of skin colors.

Boricua: (bor-EE-kwah) a name used by many people who were born in Puerto Rico or are the descendants of Puerto Ricans. The original inhabitants of Puerto Rico called the island Borikén. Other spellings include Boriquén and Borinquen.

chassé: (shah-SAY) a gliding step used in dancing in which one foot displaces the other

el huracán: (EL oo-rah-KAHN) hurricane

espejo: (es-PEH-hoh) mirror

fro: (FROH) short for Afro. The Afro is a natural hairstyle worn by Black people and people of color with lengthy, kinky hair texture styled like a halo.

jeté: (zhe-TAY) a type of jump in which a dancer extends one leg and then jumps off the floor with the other

Latinx: (lah-TEE-nekx) refers to someone with Latin American heritage. A Latinx person may be Black (Afro-Latinx) or white.

malo: (MAH-loh) bad

mano de la mano: (MAH-noh DAY LA MAH-noh) hand in hand

Nubian: (NOO-bee-in) refers to someone from or having ancestors from Nubia, an ancient region in northeast Africa along the Nile River in southern Egypt and northern Sudan

papi: (PAH-pee) daddy

pelo-city: (PEH-loh-sih-tee) a poetic term referring to the movement of hair. It rhymes with velocity.

pelo-flow: (PEH-loh FLO) hair flow

pelo-grow: (PEH-loh GRO) hair grow

peloooow: (PEH-loooow) a poetic word communicating the pain children experience when having their hair pulled

piraguas: (pee-RAH-gwahs) a Puerto Rican dessert that is made of shaved ice covered with fruit-flavored syrup and shaped like a pyramid. It is typically served in a cup with a straw.

Preciosa: (PREH-see-oh-sah) precious. It is also the title of a song that expresses love for Puerto Rico and the island's Taíno, Spanish, and Black ancestry, written by Rafael Hernández in 1937. "Preciosa" is considered the unofficial anthem of Puerto Rico.

princesa: (prihn-SAY-sah) princess

qué ves aquí: (KAY VEHS AH-kee) What do you see here?

Rudine: (roo-DEEN) Rudine is named after Dr. Rudine Sims Bishop, a children's literature scholar. Bishop has been called the mother of multicultural literature. She originated the idea that books can be mirrors, windows, and sliding glass doors—reflecting readers' own experiences, allowing them to see into the experiences of another, and permitting them to enter new places.

soy perfecto: (SOY pair-FEHK-toh) I am perfect

Taíno: (TIE-ee-noh) the Taíno were the Indigenous people of the Caribbean. They were the main inhabitants of most of Cuba, Hispaniola (what is now Haiti and the Dominican Republic), Jamaica, Puerto Rico, the Bahamas, and the northern Lesser Antilles. Descendants of the Taíno still live in the Carribean region—and beyond.

OUR HAIR STORIES

I want you to look in a mirror. Say: I am beautiful. ¡Soy perfecto! It is the truth. Touch your exquisite crown of hair. What story will your hair tell about you today?

NoNieqa Ramos

My natural hair is not the typical hair I've seen depicted as "beautiful" Latinx hair. It is bushy and frizzy and large. When I was a kid, hairdressers were at a loss and I always came home after haircuts crying at the butchery. No matter what my family told me, every image around me told me my hair was a Brillo pad. I first learned to tame it with Dep gel. I was one of those crunchy-haired girls for a decade or two. My soul mate calls my hair in its natural state a lion's mane. I love that imagery. I want every kid to fiercely love every strand of their cultural identities and all the ways that identity manifests.

Keisha Morris

I never really thought much about my hair, only that I wanted it out of the way. When I was younger, I would always gel it up and push it back into a curly poof or ask my mom to cornrow it. It wasn't until I was older that I started embracing its natural flow and curls, using products that worked with my hair instead of damaging it. As an adult, I take more pride in my hair and I no longer want it "out of the way." Now, I love how I use my hair to reflect my personality. Two-strand twists with shaved sides—I love it!